Happy St. Patrick's Day,
HELLO KITTY®

D1360089

Happy St. Patrick's Day,

HELLO KITTY®

Abrams Books for Young Readers
New York

One morning, before she even opens her eyes, Hello Kitty hears
the sound of bagpipes. The St. Patrick's Day parade!

Hello Kitty jumps out of bed and looks in her closet. A green
dress is perfect. Now all she needs is her shamrock headband.
She races downstairs to find Mama.

Doesn't Mama hear the bagpipes? They'll be late for the parade if they don't leave soon.

That's not the parade, Mama tells her. That's just Mimmy practicing in the other room.

Hello Kitty is happy she didn't miss the parade. She decides to practice her Irish jig while Mimmy plays the bagpipes. How fun!

Hello Kitty puts on her special shoes. Right knee up, now hop. Left knee up, now hop again. Keep going—faster, faster. She'd better stop practicing soon, or she'll be too tired to dance at the parade.

Besides, Hello Kitty needs to work on her St. Patrick's Day poem. She already has most of it written.

The St. Patrick's Day Parade
By Hello Kitty

Four days before spring,
It's time to wear green.
When the marching begins,
Hope you know the routine!

Won't you join the parade?
Come and dance, just a little.
Don't be afraid,
Clap along to the fiddle.

Just a wee bit o' luck
Will make the rain go,
At least till the marching ends
And we find a . . .

shamrock

pot of gold

four-leaf clover

?

Hello Kitty is still stuck on the last line. We find a—what? "Shamrock" doesn't rhyme. Neither does "pot of gold." "Four-leaf clover" won't work. What will they find at the end of the parade?

She'll have to wait to find out. Mama is calling her for breakfast. Shamrock cookies and tea! After breakfast it's time to go, even though she still hasn't finished her poem.

The drums are beating as they arrive at the parade. Hello Kitty and
Mimmy race to get to the front.

There's Fifi playing the bagpipes! Mimmy jumps in next to her. Thomas is playing the drum, and Tippy is riding his bike. Tracy is holding a giant shamrock. Dear Daniel is waving the Irish flag.

Hello Kitty smiles at her neighbors and friends along the sidelines. There's Mama! There's Papa! Everyone is cheering and waving. Jodie is riding a big float that looks like a pot of gold. Hello Kitty climbs up onto the float next to Jodie.

Hello Kitty remembers all her dance steps and feels so excited, she doesn't even notice at first when it starts to rain. Oh no! Will the parade be ruined?

As the friends round the last corner of the parade, Hello Kitty sees a red stripe in the sky up ahead. Fifi sees orange. Mimmy sees yellow. What is it?

It's a rainbow! If you look hard enough after it rains, sometimes you can see a beautiful rainbow.

The time has come for the last song before the parade ends. This one is Hello Kitty's favorite. It's about the green hills of Ireland.

After the parade, Hello Kitty and her friends go searching for the pot of gold at the end of the rainbow. But Hello Kitty has found something even better: the perfect ending to her poem!

Just a wee bit o' luck
Will make the rain go,
At least till the marching ends
And we find a **rainbow**.

Library of Congress Cataloging-in-Publication Data
Happy St. Patrick's Day, Hello Kitty / by Sanrio.
pages cm
ISBN 978-1-4197-1556-3
I. Sanrio.
PZ7.H21 2015
[E]—dc23
2014020927

Book design by Alissa Faden

Printed and bound in China
10 9 8 7 6 5 4 3 2 1

THE ART OF BOOKS SINCE 1949

115 West 18th Street
New York, NY 10011
www.abramsbooks.com